Hello!

My name is Hans. Welcome to my story.

You might know me from some of your favorite stories: "The Little Mermaid," "The Princess and the Pea," or "The Ugly Duckling."

My full name is Hans Christian. But you can call me H.C. That's what my friends call me. Plus, if we shorten my name to "H.C.," we'll have more room to write our adventure.

I am a teller of stories, specifically of fairy tales. And have I got a story for you.

I was born in Odense, Denmark, on April 2, 1805. The city is southwest of Denmark's capital, Copenhagen.

When I was young, I received a magic hat. When I put my hat on my head, I am transported to marvelous places with marvelous people. Well, for the most part. There have been some not-so-marvelous people.

But every story needs a villain.

I invite you to join me on my adventures.

So grab a hat—a baseball cap, a cowboy hat, one of those hats with a tiny propeller on top! If you don't have a hat, just use your imagination. You'll be using it a lot.

P.S. If you're wondering what part of this adventure comes from my imagination and what part comes from the real world, read "The H.C. Chronicles" at the back.

GRAB YOUR
HAT
AND GET
READY FOR
AN ADVENTURE!

Odense, Denmark: Winter is here. Its cold winds have long since blown the last leaves off the trees. The mad dash for festive presents has begun. The children bursting with energy are a sure sign that the holidays are near, as they're chased around by their frazzled parents. Who said that holidays are supposed to be joyful?

Look at this statue, H.C. What a funny look on her face!

Ha!

?

Our bus!

Quick!

Voltaire, I'll never understand why people always have to rush.

H.C.?

What are you doing?

My house!

I'm sure there's a logical explanation for all this.

What's going on?

Pfff!

Grr!

Walt Disney?

To what do we owe the pleasure?

Have you heard the latest?

No, but it must be better than the destruction of my house.

You mean the restoration of your house, Andersen!

Restoration?

Yes, they're renovating your childhood home.

Why would they do that?

To honor his accomplishments!

Oh no, my manuscript!

My manuscript!

Wait!

What are you talking about, H.C.?

My hidden manuscript!

Whoa! I smell suspense and adventure.

And where is it?

It's...

in my house...

But where?

I hid it a long time ago, but I forget where.

Tell us the story of this manuscript from the beginning. That could jog your memory, couldn't it?

Yes! Tell us, H.C.!

I'm sure you're right. Let's see, how did it go again?

It all started in a cold December, even colder than today. I was eight years old and my best friend, Karen, had gone to the orphanage.

My parents couldn't afford to take her in. But we were still always together...

H.C.!

As I may have told you before, Karen had helped me to recover my magic hat, stolen by the evil innkeeper. From that moment on, we were inseparable.

The hat had been given to me by my grandfather. It was a real magical one! The hat, not my grandfather. Then again...

Karen and I had an amazing summer full of laughs and adventure. But when winter came, life lost its sparkle for Karen. Her clothes were ragged...

Her only shoes let in the cold and damp...

Why don't you come inside?

You'll catch cold.

Nothing interesting happens inside.

Nothing interesting? Do you mean to say I've never told you the story of how Grandfather's ship was attacked by the terrible pirate Firebeard?

Yippeeeee, a story!

My father told wonderful stories. He could transport us to the seven seas or to the middle of a great desert, all while working on his shoes.

He was my first source of inspiration. It's partly thanks to him that I became a storyteller.

Thank you for the tea.

Those shoes don't look very suitable for walking in the snow.

You're right, but it's better than going barefoot.

Wait there, I'll be right back!

Where's he going, H.C.?

I don't know...

???

Papa?

It's an old pair, but I'm sure they'll keep out the water. They're yours, if you want them.

My father may not have been rich. But when it came to generosity, he had a heart the size of the Himalayas.

7

Karen was so happy with her new red shoes that she lost no time in putting them on and wearing them all over town.

Look, a poster for a play!

THEATER AUDITION

What does it say?

Um... well...

It's in French. It says they need actors for their new play.

Really?!

That's perfect for us.

If you think you can do it, I wish you good luck!

Thanks!

8

WINTER PLAY AUDITION THIS WEEK ONLY

So, it's real?

Yes, it seems to be an audition.

Do you really think we should?

Well... how do we get in?

Through the front door!

Oh, of course, through the front door.

Are you nervous? Why aren't you going in?

...I'm right behind you.

Phew!!!

As you can see, there is no one here. How could you think the local peasants would be interested in acting?

?

Come now, dear. We will find a solution. Our young actress will arrive. I can sense it...

9

Humph! I could easily play my part and the young girl's. It's not necessary to find another actress.

But you wouldn't have time to change during the performance!

?

Excuses, always excuses!

What?! There she is, our young star!

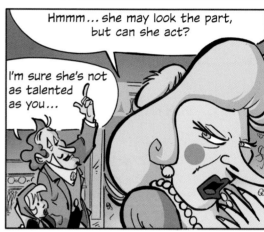

Hmmm... she may look the part, but can she act?

I'm sure she's not as talented as you...

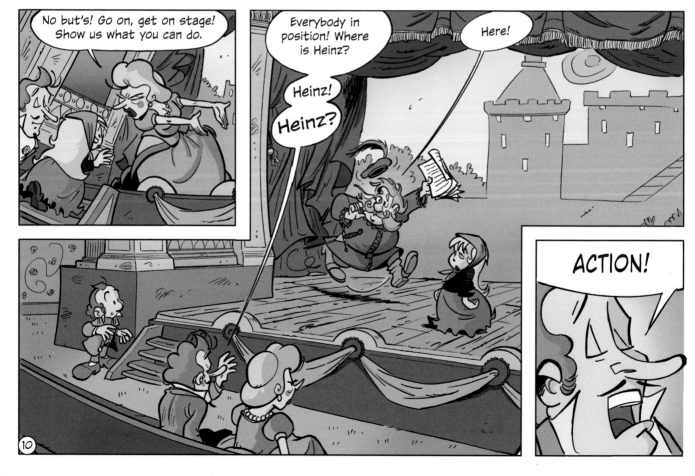

No but's! Go on, get on stage! Show us what you can do.

Everybody in position! Where is Heinz?

Heinz!

Heinz?

Here!

ACTION!

You are wonderful, truly magnificent!

We're only missing one more person to play the pine tree and then we're set!

Let me play the pine tree. I will be your trunk... your needles!

Please! Give him a chance!

Do you know him?

He's my best friend!

You are too small to play the part. A pine tree must be majestic, grand. What would the audience say if, instead of a king of the forest, I gave them a shrub?

But it's the moment I've been waiting for all my life. I can do it. You'll see!

...Fine. Come back tomorrow for the dress rehearsal. If we haven't found anyone, we'll see what we can do...

Thank you!

Yes, yes. Run along now.

Your wish is my command, gentle sir.

Are you coming?

I have to learn my lines for tomorrow's performance. Heinz is helping me.

We shall meet again tomorrow, dear lady.

Yes, noble prince.

12

Look, it's H.C.!

Look at your big nose, like our snowman's!

H.C., do you recognize him?

PLOP

POF!

Ha! It's you: half snowman, half Mr. Potato Head!

Go ahead and laugh! Starting tomorrow, I'm going to be a famous actor. We'll see who has the last laugh.

Your Excellency, are you thinking of reciting your verses...

...with that schnoz? Ha! Ha! Ha!

Ha, your nose!

Ha! Ha!

It'll be okay. It'll be okay. I'm sure it'll be okay.

13

That night, I told my parents about my day with Karen. And that I was going to play the pine tree.

Ha! Our son, an actor! What great news! It's obvious who the boy gets it from!

Why don't you say anything, Mama?

I don't think it's a good idea...

Why, Mama?

It's not your fault, but I broke a mirror today...

Mama...

It's a bad omen. I can feel it. It's going to be a disaster.

Let him go! He might never get another opportunity like this!

But what about the mirror?

It's just a mirror...

You don't understand. It will bring him bad luck!

That night, I wasn't able to sleep. What if my mother was right? What if I wasn't good enough? What if I really was nervous, as Karen had pointed out? What if...

The next morning, I woke up very stressed.

Hello, H.C.!

Hi, Karen...

You don't look very happy.

I don't think I'll get the part.

Nobody else showed up, so the part is still available!

What? I'm going to get the part!

What are you talking about?

You're still too small.

But you don't have anybody else, right? Right?

The day has only just begun.

Wait!

?

If I wear my hat during the performance, I'll be at least a head taller!

What?

Yes, this hat right here!

If I give you a chance, will you promise to stop bugging me?

I promise.

Good. Get to work.

I was sure of it. Bravo, H.C.!

Did you say hello to Heinz?

No, not yet!

Heinz is German. He still can't speak our language very well, but he's trying.

Hello! How do you do?

Hello, Heinz! I am very pleased to meet you.

All I had to do was learn my lines, but we got to chatting and I didn't see what time it was.

H.C.! You're on stage in three minutes!

Oh no! I didn't learn my lines. What am I going to do?

Get on stage!

Don't worry, it'll be okay. I'll help you.

If you can help me out, hat, it's now or never. I really need you.

What's the matter?

What do you mean?

Well, you look so sad!

Look at how I look. Isn't that a good reason to be sad?

Pierre, he isn't following the script.

Let him continue!

My branches are tangled, my bark is falling off. I'm not nice to look at.

Do you feel... ugly?

Yes, exactly. I'm ugly!

I know how you feel. People make fun of me. All the ducks on the farm call me the ugly duckling!

Sniff. Sniff.

You're not ugly! I think you're rather cute!

You're the first person to tell me that.

Thank you!

CUT

Magnificent! That was magnificent!

I've always wanted to find an actor like you!

Ahhh! I've never seen such talent!

Pierre, I'm taking the part of the little girl.

What?

???

???

Huh? What? You're not serious...

I get the part or **I go.**

Fine. But then the young lady gets your part.

?

Yes! Yes!

In the meantime, why don't we go talk paperwork? The contracts await, my young new friend.

Hee! Hee!

Here they are.

To be a real actor, you must sign real contracts. Here's a quill and some ink.

Sign at the bottom on the right, my boy.

Why are some letters smaller than others?

Oh, that? That's normal. It's to keep the contract from being boring. It's much prettier with a variety of letter heights. Now sign, and your dream will finally come true!

19

Karen, you don't look well. Is it because of your new part?

I don't know if I can do it. I have to learn a whole new set of lines. tomorrow.

It'll be okay. I believe in you!

Thanks! That makes me feel better.

You'll be perfect.

The next morning, I hurried to be at the theater on time. Pierre was explaining some details of the scenery to Heinz.

No, no, no, that won't do!

H.C! How are you this morning?

I'm excellent, thank you!

Are you ready for tonight? It's the grand opening! I'm expecting the same performance from you as yesterday!

Yes, but...

Excellent! We agree then. I have to go now, I have a pile of work to do.

H.C., can you help me rehearse? I spent all night learning my lines.

We worked hard that day and succeeded in memorizing our lines. Before we knew it, it was time! We were going on stage!

H.C., your costume is ready. Karen, get ready. You're on soon!

Are you ready?

As ready as I'll ever be. I'll see you on stage!

H.C., you have to put on your costume. Put your head through there.

Can I get my hat through there?

Hat? Oh no!

But I need my hat! Without my hat, it'll be a disaster!

What?

My hat!

It's too small!

H.C., you're up. Get on stage!

Go on, hurry!

You must mean that **YOU** have a funny nose!

Uh...

Oh...yes, of course. I have a funny nose and you...

...

SCRASJ

You... uh... you...

That's enough!

?

Oh no! The curtain! Quickly!

Why do these things always happen to me? My mother was right, I should've listened to her...

As for you, this is all your fault!

All I wanted was to be an actor! Why are you like this? All you're good for is making me daydream, then twisting reality, so that I end up making a bigger fool of myself!

That night in bed, I thought about Karen and what she must think of me now...

H.C., how could you do this to me?

How?

I'm sorry, Karen. I didn't mean to, but I'm going to fix this.

I promise.

And I'm going to start right now!

I decided to write my very first manuscript in honor of Karen. I hoped she would forgive me for ruining her theatrical debut...

Let's see. How do you start a manuscript? It can't be so hard!

Hmm...

What if I gave you one last chance?

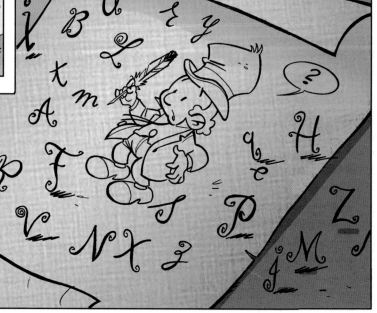

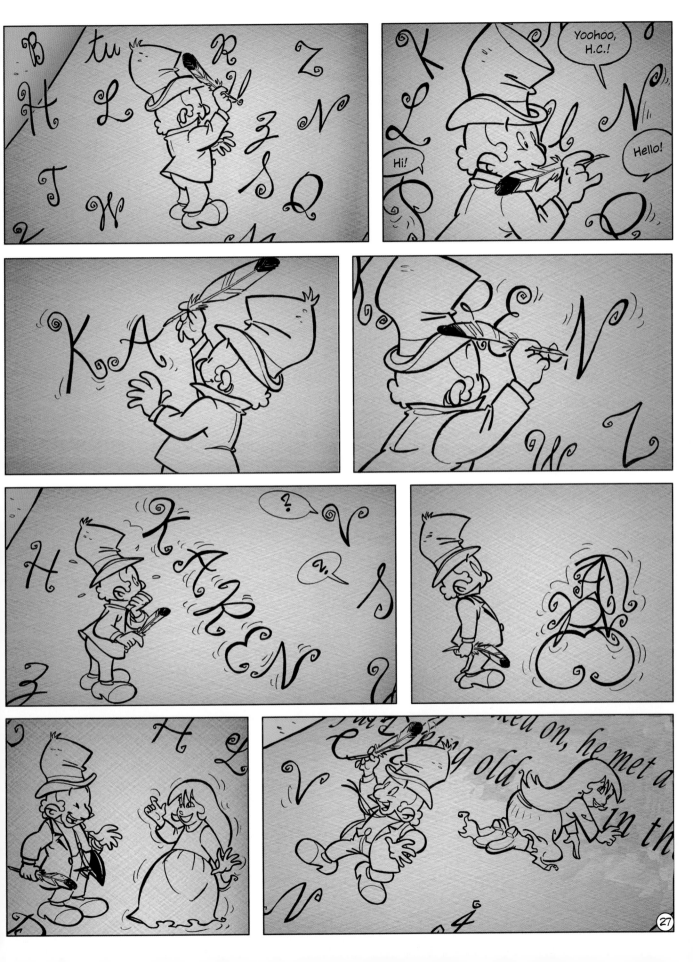

Attack!

Hahaha!

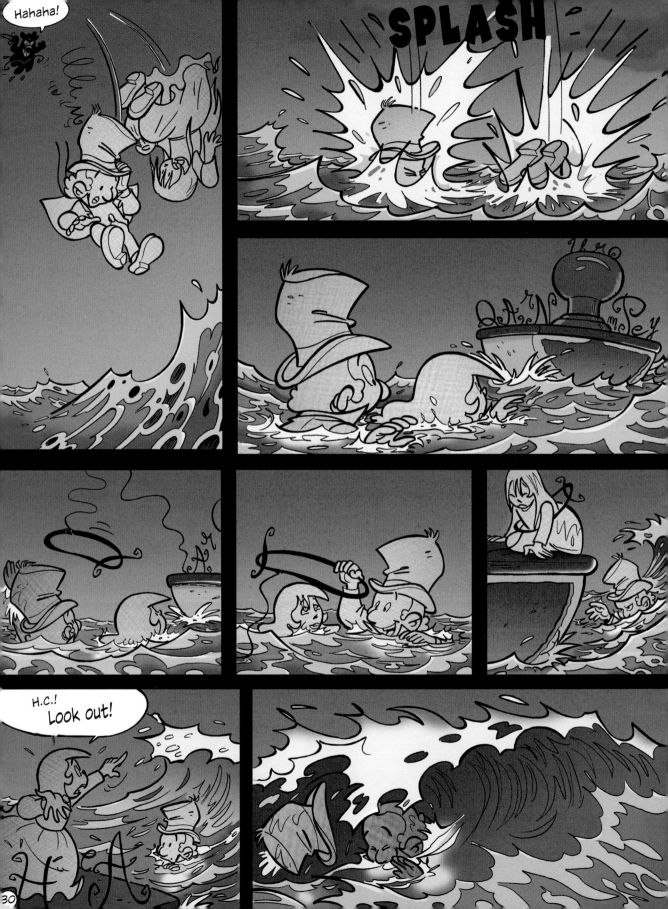

Oh, my head!
I feel all woozy!

???

Did I really write all that?

This is amazing!
It's about Karen ...

I'm going to run and show her.
I'm sure she'll forgive me.

Oops!

???

I'm sorry!
I didn't see you there.
I'm bringing...

YOU!

Come back! I'll show you!

???

H.C.! What are you doing here? What's wrong?

I... I... wrote you a manuscript...

Show me!

I dropped it when I bumped into Pierre, and I don't dare go back to get it!

I'll take care of it. Come with us!

???

What are you doing here? Pierre!

That's my manuscript! I'll leave, but I'd like it back first.

Your manuscript? One doesn't give a manuscript to a little child like you.

It's my manuscript! I wrote it.

What! That's too funny. Pierre!

Why are you yelling? What's going on?

You again!

Why didn't you show this to me?

I hope you weren't planning to save this little jewel for someone else...

Huh?

Of course not, but...

Then prove it! Give me the lead role in this play.

But...

Goodbye!

Wait! The part is yours! It's all for you!

But it's Hans's manuscript. You can't give it away like that. Plus, he wrote it for Karen.

33

Come on, Heinz, be realistic. You don't think a mere boy could write such a manuscript, do you? He obviously stole it!

But...

Enough "but's"! One more word and you're fired!

???

HABS

He took my manuscript!

Huh, what?

Bring me back that manuscript, Pierre, or I'm leaving this theater.

I'll get it!

Oh, no! Pierre is too fast for me!

...the hat!

Aaaaahh!

Aaaaahhh!

37

Ha! It's just a cow.

I warned you. I want that part!

I don't want to hear any more about H.C. and his manuscript! ENOUGH!

Pack my bags. I'm leaving this place forever.

Okay!

Enough. I'll recover the manuscript.

Karen!

Z

Karen, I'm thinking of acquiring H.C.'s manuscript in exchange for cash.

Really? WOW!

Of course! But for that, I'll need to know where he lives...

Karen believed Pierre. The next day, when I saw her again, she told me about their conversation and said that she'd given him my address. But he never came by. Had he given up his plan of acquiring my manuscript? On top of that, I...

Oh my!

I remember now...ohhhh mischievous memory! I had to tell you the whole story before I could remember!

Upon returning home the day that Pierre chased me, I stepped on a loose floorboard.

Creak!

And while I was replacing it, I got an idea: many people were after this manuscript, and giving it to Karen would surely bring her a lot of trouble. While I waited for an opportunity to give it to her, I decided...

...to hide it there, under the floor!

I remember that the next day, Karen told me Pierre had never returned from visiting me. She added that the little troupe had decided to go to Italy...

...and take her with them! I was very sad, but Karen promised they would come back to Denmark soon, and that she would write me as often as she could. Heinz and the actress apparently became great friends...

?

I can't believe it's still here after all these years...my very first manuscript!

Uh... H.C.... there's nothing here!

What do you mean?! But this is where I left it! It has to be here!

39

Unbelievable! There's a giant hole under the floor!

Maybe your manuscript fell into it?

Aargg!!!

My goodness!

There!

A skeleton!

Let's not lose our heads. It's probably a sewage worker who had an accident. We are in the sewer, aren't we?

HAHAHAHAHA SNIRRRLL FLLLLL SNIRRF

41

Who are you?
Is that you, H.C.?

My manuscript! What are you doing with my manuscript? Why are you here?

I didn't think I'd ever see anybody again. Especially not you, and especially not as a ghost! I just wanted to borrow it, read it...

How did you end up down here?

First, I tricked Karen into telling me where I could find you...

Yes, yes!
I know that part!
What next?

42

So I went to your house. I still didn't know how I would get my hands on the manuscript...

...but luck was on my side. Peeking through the window, I saw you hide it under the floorboards. Now all I had to do was go inside and steal the precious document.

I was just about to do it when a couple arrived, most likely your parents...

I had to think of another plan fast. That's when a crazy idea came to me...

43

It may have been foolish, but I was obsessed with possessing the manuscript. Loosening the rocks under your house took me hours...

Just as I was about to get through, the wall caved in suddenly, and I was crushed under the rocks...

But when I awoke, I found the precious manuscript right there in front of me. All I had to do was grab it.

I took it and started reading. I was captivated. A feeling of intense joy and happiness overcame me, and for a moment I forgot everything else...

When I was leaving, I noticed my earthly vessel crushed under an enormous rock.

?

And I realized that I was going to be a prisoner of the sewers for all eternity...

No!!!

SNIFFFF!

Whisper. Whisper. Whisper.

We've talked it over...

I think we've found a way to get you out of here.

The next day:

Hey, look at this!

45

Hey, where did this come from?

What is it?

It looks like paper.

We should probably contact the museum.

I want to know who made this hole.

The city of Odense is the proud home of a museum dedicated to the most famous Dane in the whole world: Hans Christian Andersen. Most of his manuscripts are on display there. All his original works are known and catalogued there. That's why today's surprise is immense:

H.C. ANDERSEN MUSEUM

A new manuscript!?

This is a historical event!

What about my hole?

Your discovery is unprecedented!

And what about Pierre, you may be asking?

My forgiveness was enough to free him from the sewer. He became a guide at the museum, which is visited by countless living beings and ghosts. They come to hear the story of my life and admire my works.

Allow me to tell you the incredible story of the hidden manuscript, in which I played a humble role.

THE H.C. CHRONICLES

While my grandfather gave me a magical hat that unlocks my imagination, I did not imagine all of the people in this book.

You will now see the real people and places that inspired my stories.

The people and places in my stories have, in turn, inspired other stories. People have created ballets, movies, fairy tales, and theme-park rides. I never imagined that my words would be translated into delightful rides to be enjoyed between ice cream and other festival foods.

My stories have even been made into plays. I wonder if Pierre would want to direct the play. I am sure that the actress in this book would want to play the main character, whoever that character is.

Although my fairy tales and these other creative endeavors have been centuries and countries apart, we have all been affected by the world around us.

So be sure to open your eyes and try new things. If you've never been in a play, try it! Although I would not recommend trying to anger a theater director.

WHO'S WHO

Even though Voltaire and I thought the statue had a funny face, it was actually quite boo-tiful! Do you know much about my two ghostly companions?

VOLTAIRE

Voltaire (1694-1778) was not this man's real name. And it wasn't a case like mine of going by H.C. rather than Hans Christian. "Voltaire" was the pen name of Francois Marie Arouet. He was a French author and philosopher. Like I do in some of my fairy tales, Voltaire's works explore the nature of good and evil.

WALT DISNEY

One of the ghosts in this story was Walt Disney (1901-1966). He was a famous movie producer. Along with creating such cartoon film characters as Mickey Mouse and Donald Duck, Disney is famous for creating theme parks.

In 1939, Disney released *The Ugly Duckling.* The movie was inspired by my fairy tale "The Ugly Duckling."

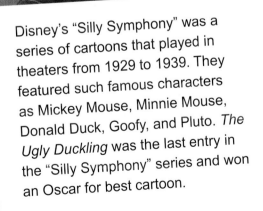

Disney's "Silly Symphony" was a series of cartoons that played in theaters from 1929 to 1939. They featured such famous characters as Mickey Mouse, Minnie Mouse, Donald Duck, Goofy, and Pluto. *The Ugly Duckling* was the last entry in the "Silly Symphony" series and won an Oscar for best cartoon.

WHAT'S WHAT

TIVOLI

In 1843, I saw one of the most marvelous things I had ever seen: Tivoli Gardens in Copenhagen. For months, I had watched the glorious garden be constructed. For months, I heard the musicians warming up their instruments. For months, I had dreamed of that wonderland. On opening day, it seemed as if all of Copenhagen was waiting to enter the amusement park. Once inside, I was awestruck. There were restaurants, cafes, a theater, a merry-go-round and flowers—oh the flowers! The entire park twinkled with beautiful little lights. I was so inspired by the grand gardens that I knew I wanted to create a fairy tale that existed in a world such as that. I wrote "The Nightingale." It is the story of an emperor and talented bird who live amongst gardens and flowers and lights as beautiful as those at Tivoli.

The Camel Trail is one of my favorite rides at Tivoli. Unlike the camel in my adventure, the camel at Tivoli doesn't nibble at you.

A pantomime show called "The Ugly Chicken" being performed at Tivoli. Children from the Tivoli Ballet School created the roles.

DISNEY PARKS

Walt Disney is famous for creating theme parks. In 1955, he opened Disneyland in Anaheim, California. Tivoli inspired his magnificent theme park. Disney made many trips to Copenhagen to study Tivoli. He wanted Disneyland to have a similar atmosphere. Many of the attractions at Disneyland are based on Disney films.

And some rides at Tivoli are based on my fairy tales. For example, on the Flying Trunk ride (named after my fairy tale), park-goers sit in a trunk and travel through several scenes from my fairy tales.

My fairy tales have inspired rides all over the world, particularly at Disney parks. Frozen was inspired by my story "The Snow Queen." At the bottom, a parade in Disneyland Paris features "The Little Mermaid."

FUNABASHI ANDERSEN PARK

Funabashi, Japan, is a sister city of Odense, Denmark, my hometown. The Funabashi Andersen Park opened in honor of its sister city's famous resident: me! The park's zones are designed for people of all ages. The Fairy Tale Hill Zone is my favorite. There, visitors can see windmills, a fairy tale museum, and a statue of me.

A building is modeled after Danish architecture. The park features a statue of one of my most famous characters, the little mermaid.

MY FAIRY TALES

When I was begging to play the pine tree, the theater director said I was too small to play the king of the forest. He said I wasn't majestic. That is the fear of the main character in my fairy tale "The Pine Tree" (it is also sometimes called "The Fir Tree"). This is a tale of a pine tree always looking to the future, rather than being in the present.

Did you know that my fairy tales have been translated into more than 120 languages?

THE PINE TREE

A small pine tree grew in a forest with its forest friends. Swallows swirled above its head. Rabbits hopped over its roots. But it did not like this. For it wished to be as grand as the tallest pine trees in the forest. The pine tree did not take pleasure in the sunshine. Instead, it wished to speed up time.

When the tall pine trees were cut down, the small pine tree asked the storks where the trees went. "They are made into tall masts," said the storks. "Oh, wow. How I want to be a tall mast …" thought the pine tree. "Be glad that you are young," whispered the sun's rays. "Enjoy your strength and the pleasure of being alive."

More tall pine trees were taken away. "Where are they going?" the pine tree asked. "They are going inside warm living rooms. They will be decorated with silver and gold," the swallows replied. The tall pine trees were being transformed into beautiful Christmas trees!

"Oh, to be decorated with silver and gold …," thought the small pine tree.

One day, the small pine tree was taken from the forest. Its wish came true!

It was taken into a warm living room.

It was decorated with silver and gold.

It was the centerpiece in the festive celebration.

And then it was thrown into the dark attic, never to be used again.

There it sat. Mice burrowed in its branches and listened to the pine tree's fairy tale. The mice asked the pine tree about the forest. As the pine tree described its friends and the sun's golden rays, it longed for its home. It longed for the place it had wished to leave.

When spring came, the pine tree was taken from the attic and placed outside. It was cut into kindling and placed in the stove. It warmed the family, and it longed for the forest.

THE UGLY DUCKLING

This fairy tale holds a special place in my heart, for it is the story of my life.

A mama bird waited for her last duckling to hatch. When he emerged, the mama duck yelled, "What a creature! He is so big and ugly!" Even though he performs all of his duck duties well—namely swimming—he is forced to leave the pond. The other animals don't want to be by such an ugly duckling. As he travels, animals continue to say how ugly he is. When he spots a group of beautiful birds, he thinks, "Oh, to be a beautiful bird." After a long winter, the duckling sees his reflection in the pond. He realizes he was not a duck—he was a beautiful bird. He was a swan. He becomes the most beautiful swan in the whole pond.

WHAT WOULD YOU DO?

There are many morals to this story. In particular, it is a story about kindness. In this case, there is a lack of kindness. Be sure to celebrate each other's differences, for they are what make the world an exciting place. We must encourage everyone to be their best selves. How will you do your part?

THE RED SHOES

My father gave Karen a pair of red shoes to protect her feet from the cold. These red shoes are from my fairy tale "The Red Shoes." In this story, a poor girl named Karen is taken in by an older woman after Karen's mother dies. When it's time to get a new pair of shoes, Karen spots a beautiful pair of red shoes. She gets the red shoes and wears them all the time—particularly at times when red shoes are not appropriate.

The red shoes start to control Karen. She can't take them off!

She dances through the city and out into the forest. As I write in my tale, "Dance she must, and dance she did. The shoes carried her across fields and meadows, through nettles and briars that tore her feet so they bled." Karen asks someone to cut off her feet—red shoes and all. They follow her orders. She spends the rest of her days living a simple, generous life.

Now, this was not the fate of Karen in this book. She traveled with the acting troupe.

The ballerina Moira Shearer dancing in the movie The Red Shoes (1948). The ballet is based on my fairy tale. How I would have loved to be a dancer ...

Can you think of any other movie that had red shoes?

Remember when I escaped from the evil theater director via a trunk? Well, that is based on my fairy tale "The Flying Trunk." A merchant loses all of his money and is gifted with a trunk. If the merchant pressed on the lock, the trunk would fly. He flies to Turkey and falls in love with a princess. She asks him to tell her and her parents a story. Here is his tale:

THE FLYING TRUNK

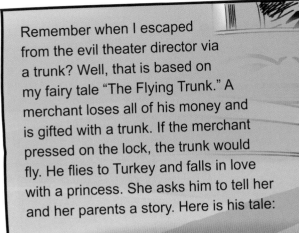

There was once a bundle of matches that were exceedingly proud of their high descent. Their genealogical tree, that is, a large pine tree from which they had been cut, was at one time a large, old tree in the wood. The matches now lay between a tinderbox and an old iron saucepan, and were talking about their youthful days. "Ah! Then we grew on the green boughs, and were as green as they; every morning and evening we were fed with diamond drops of dew. Whenever the sun shone, we felt his warm rays, and the little birds would relate stories to us as they sung. We knew that we were rich, for the other trees only wore their green dress in summer, but our family were able to array themselves in green, summer and winter. But the wood-cutter came, like a great revolution, and our family fell under the axe. The head of the house obtained a situation as mainmast in a very fine ship, and can sail round the world when he will. The other branches of the family were taken to different places, and our office now is to kindle a light for common people. This is how such high-born people as we came to be in a kitchen."

"Mine has been a very different fate," said the iron pot, which stood by the matches. "From my first entrance into the world, I

have been used to cooking and scouring. I am the first in this house, when anything solid or useful is required. My only pleasure is to be made clean and shining after dinner, and to sit in my place and have a little sensible conversation with my neighbors. All of us, excepting the water bucket, which is sometimes taken into the courtyard, live here together within these four walls. We get our news from the market basket, but he sometimes tells us very unpleasant things about the people and the government. Yes, and one day an old pot was so alarmed, that he fell down and was broken to pieces."

"You are talking too much," said the tinderbox, and the steel struck against the flint until some sparks flew out, crying, "We want a merry evening, don't we?"

"Yes, of course," said the matches, "let us talk about those who are the highest born."

"No, I don't like to be always talking of what we are," remarked the saucepan. "Let us think of some other amusement; I will begin. We will tell something that has happened to ourselves. That will be very easy, and interesting as well. On the Baltic Sea, near the Danish shore—"

"What a pretty commencement!" said the plates. "We shall all like that story, I am sure."

"Yes. Well, in my youth, I lived in a quiet family, where the furniture was polished, the floors scoured, and clean curtains put up every fortnight."

"What an interesting way you have of relating a story," said the carpet

broom. "It is easy to perceive that you have been a great deal in society, there is something so pure runs through what you say."

"That is quite true," said the water bucket. He made a spring with joy, and splashed some water on the floor.

Then the saucepan went on with his story, and the end was as good as the beginning. The plates rattled with pleasure, and the carpet broom brought some green parsley out of the dust hole and crowned the saucepan, for he knew it would vex the others. He thought, "If I crown him today he will crown me tomorrow."

"Now, let us have a dance," said the fire tongs. Then how they danced and stuck up one leg in the air. The chair-cushion in the corner burst with laughter when she saw it.

"Shall I be crowned now?" asked the fire tongs. So the broom found another wreath for the tongs.

"They were only common people after all," thought the matches. The tea urn was now asked to sing, but she said she had a cold, and could not sing without boiling heat. They all thought this was affectation, and because she did not wish to sing except in the parlor, when on the table with the grand people.

In the window sat an old quill pen, with which the maid generally wrote. There was nothing remarkable about the pen, except that it had been dipped too deeply in the ink, but it was proud of that.

"If the tea urn won't sing," said the pen, "she can leave it alone. There is a nightingale in a cage who can sing. She has not been taught much, certainly, but we need not say anything this evening about that."

"I think it highly improper," said the tea kettle, who was kitchen

singer, and half-brother to the tea urn, "that a rich foreign bird should be listened to here. Is it patriotic? Let the market basket decide what is right."

"I certainly am vexed," said the basket. "Inwardly vexed, more than anyone can imagine. Are we spending the evening properly? Would it not be more sensible to put the house in order? If each were in his own place I would lead a game; this would be quite another thing."

"Let us act a play," they all said. At the same moment the door opened, and the maid came in. Then not one stirred; they all remained quite still; yet, at the same time, there was not a single pot amongst them who had not a high opinion of himself and of what he could do if he chose.

"Yes, if we had chosen," they each thought, "we might have spent a very pleasant evening."

The maid lit the matches. Dear me, how they sputtered and blazed up!

"Now then," they thought, "everyone will see that we are the first. How we shine; what a light we give!" Even while they spoke their light went out.

Can you think of any other movie in which the ordinary objects come to life?

MY MUSEUM

At the end of this wonderful book, there is an image of the H.C. Andersen Museum. That is a real museum! You can travel to my hometown of Odense, Denmark, to better understand my life.

Museum goers can see my childhood home. It is still a beautiful yellow color. The inside of the house is very bare. Although my parents could not afford to fill the cheery house with luxurious fabrics and ornate furniture, we were happy. I especially liked to spend time in the garden. My surroundings fostered my imagination and exploration. Maybe you will be inspired there, too! I would not recommend trying to skip the line by going through the sewers. We all know how that turns out.

My childhood home in Odense. Visit to see if you find any other stories under a loose floorboard.

I liked to have pens and paper on my desk. What do you like to keep on your desk? Markers? Notebooks? Snacks?

This area is called the "Workshop." You can see some furniture and objects from my home. I lived in the lovely district of Nyhavn in Copenhagen.

People sit by the water in which a boat inspired by "The Steadfast Tin Soldier" floats. The paper boat is located in the Fairy Tale Garden.

This Hans Christian Andersen statue is made up of Lego pieces. You can find this in LEGOLAND in Billund, Denmark. The park is just a train ride away from the museum.

Created and illustrated by
Thierry Capezzone

Written by
Jan Rybka

Directed by Tom Evans
Designed by Brenda Tropinski
Illustration colored by Jonas P. Sonne
The H.C. Chronicles written by Madeline King
Photo edited by Rosalia Bledsoe
Proofread by Nathalie Strassheim
Manufacturing led by Anne Fritzinger

World Book, Inc.
180 North LaSalle Street, Suite 900
Chicago, Illinois 60601
USA

For information about other World Book print and digital publications, please go to
www.worldbook.com or call 1-800-WORLDBK (967-5325).

For information about sales to schools and libraries,
call 1-800-975-3250 (United States) or 1-800-837-5365 (Canada).

Library of Congress Cataloging-in-Publication Data for this volume has been applied for.

The Adventures of Young H.C. Andersen
ISBN: 978-0-7166-0958-2 (set, hc.)

The Adventures of Young H.C. Andersen and the Forgotten Manuscript
ISBN: 978-0-7166-0960-5 (hc.)

Also available as:
ISBN: 978-0-7166-0965-0 (e-book)

Printed in the United States of America
by CG Book Printers, North Mankato, Minnesota
1st printing March 2020

www.worldbook.com

Museets rekonstruktion af kuglposten under en køretur i 1956.